E FICTION VAI

Vail, Rachel.

Jibberwillies at night

Withdrawn

**Please check all items for damages
before leaving the Library.
Thereafter you will be held
responsible for all injuries
to items beyond reasonable wear.**

Helen M. Plum Memorial Library

Lombard, Illinois

A daily fine will be charged for
overdue materials.

OCT   2008

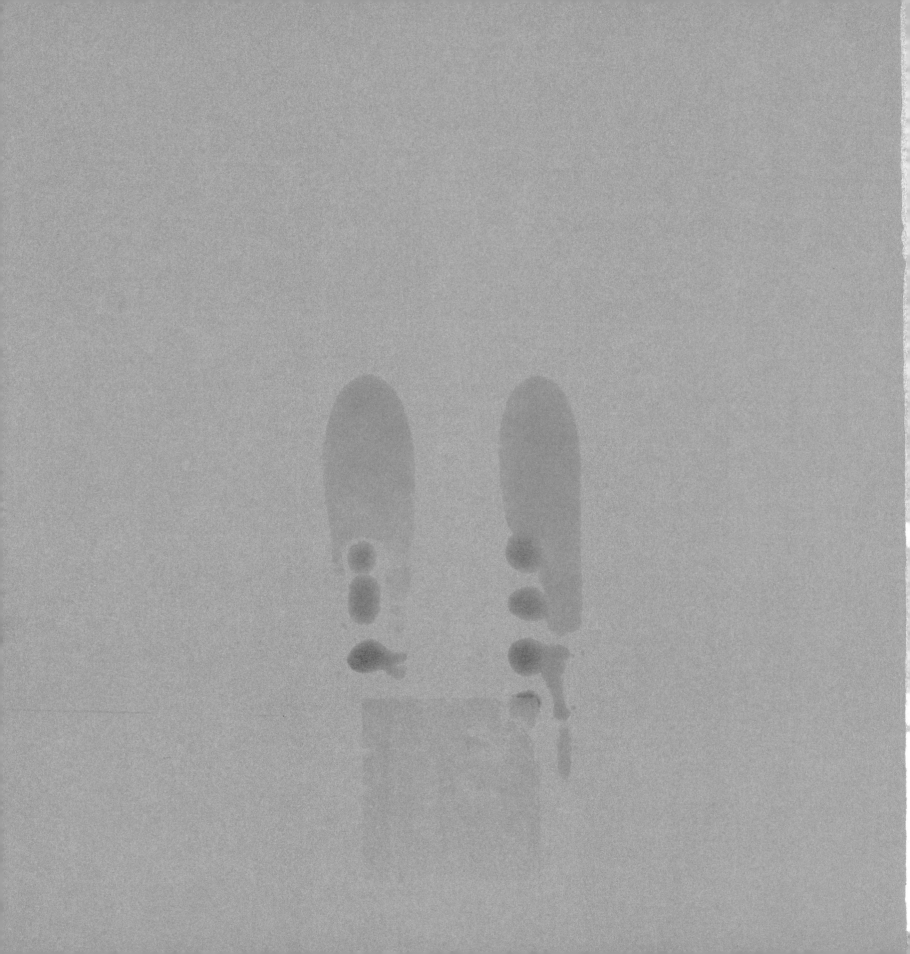

Jibberwillies
at Night

by
RACHEL VAIL

Illustrated by
YUMI HEO

SCHOLASTIC PRESS   NEW YORK

E
FICTION
VAI

● Library of Congress Cataloging-in-Publication Data Vail, Rachel. ● Jibberwillies at night / by Rachel Vail ; illustrated by Yumi Heo. p. cm. ● Summary: Katie is almost always happy, but sometimes at night, when the Jibberwillies come and scare her, her mother must catch them in a bucket and throw them out the window before Katie can fall asleep. [1. Fear—Fiction. 2. Bedtime—Fiction.] I. Heo, Yumi, ill. II. Title. PZ7.V1916Ji 2008 ● [E—dc22 2007034087 ISBN-13: 978-0-439-42070-9 ISBN-10: 0-439-42070-9 s10 9 8 7 6 5 4 3 2 1 08 09 10 11 12 Printed in Singapore 46 First edition, October 2008

The text type was set in VAG Rounded Bold and Ad Lib ● The display type was set in Ad Lib

The illustrations were done in ((tk)) ● Book design by Kristina Albertson

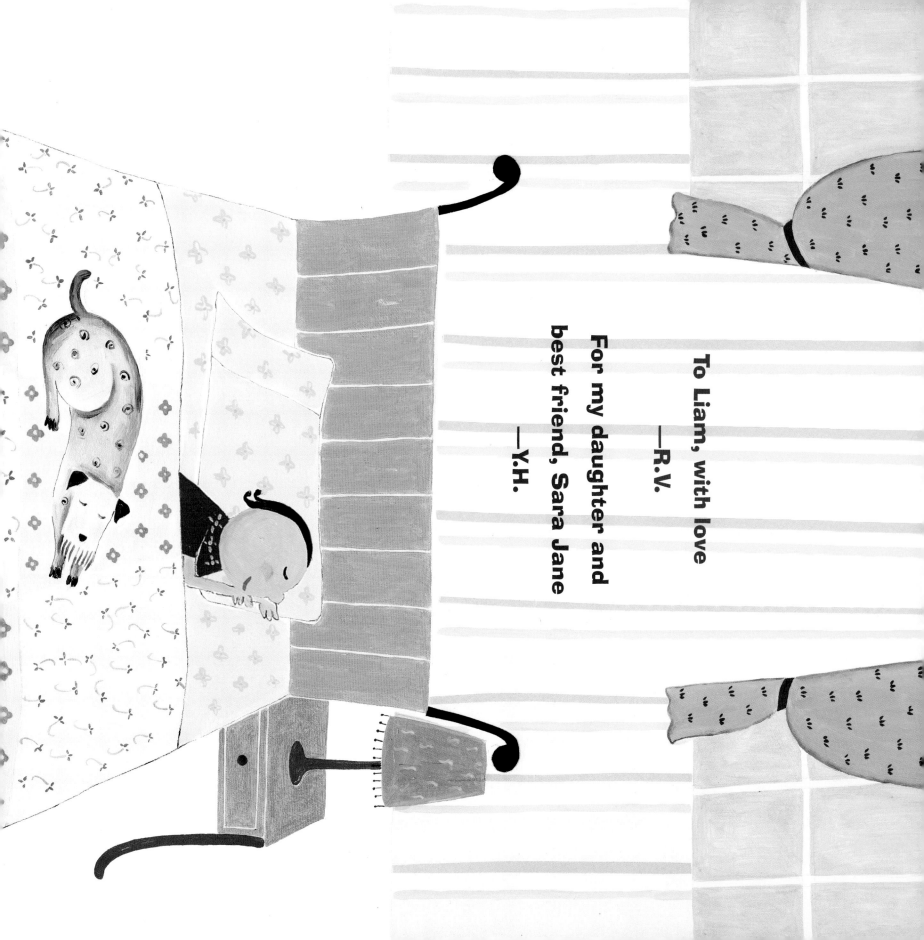

To Liam, with love

—R.V.

For my daughter and
best friend, Sara Jane

—Y.H.

My name is **Katie Honors** and I'm a really happy kid.

When the sun comes in my window,

I smile before I even open my eyes.

My friends yell

"Katie! Katie!"
as soon as they see me.
and then we
We jump around and
get busy with blocks or
markers or pretending.

I sometimes **twirl** instead of walking.

I love to play quietly by myself
or to cuddle up with my mom or dad.

My little brother squishes in sometimes and makes it crowded, but I don't mind that kind of crowded, too much.

Sometimes I even like it.

At night I put on

my **soft** pajamas

and brush my **teeth**

with my

purple toothbrush

that I picked out myself

and then sometimes

I **dance,**

and later

when it's lights-out,

I get my **kisses** and my book

and curl up with my blanket

and my dog, Vanilla,

and sometimes I can

just comfortable myself

right to sleep.

But sometimes the

JIBBERWILLIES

come.

I whisper bravely, "Go away."

They don't.

I scrunch up tight
and try to think of nice things,
like ice cream and rubber bands.

Nothing nice can get past the
JIBBERWILLIES.
They fill my room.
I can't get away.
Even in my special corner,
they find me.

"What's wrong?" asks my mother.

Under my blanket, I whisper,
"JIBBERWILLIES."

My mother kneels beside me.
"You want to talk about them?" she asks.

I am crying. It is too hard.

"Okay," says my mother.

"How about if you

just catch those

JIBBERWILLIES

in a bucket, so they won't bother you anymore tonight?"

I am frightened but my mother nods, so I try to catch them.

ever got on with

The JIBBERWILLIES

are too fast for my bucket, too slippery.

She thought I could catch them.
She was wrong.

I can't.

My mother tries to hug me, but
I am too slippery, too.

"I have an idea," says my mother.
"If you just say the JIBBERWILLIES out loud," she whispers,
"I'll catch them in the bucket."

I think about that, down under my bed, and ask,
"Will you throw them out the window?"

"If you want me to," she says.

I want her to.
I close my eyes and cover my ears and
I say the JIBBERWILLIES fast in the dark of my room.

The **JIBBERWILLIES** jibber above us.
I curl tight below the triangle of my mother's arm-wing.

I
am
small
under
that
wing,
and
safe.

My mother stands up and catches the

JIBBERWILLIES
in the bucket.

She opens my window.

I lean on her

while she throws the

JIBBERWILLIES out.

I wave good-bye as the

JIBBERWILLIES

get smaller

and smaller,

until there's

only sky.

We close the window. I yawn.

My mother tucks me softly into my bed.

I close my eyes and

comfortable myself to sleep.